Rabén & Sjögren Stockholm

Translation copyright © 1991 by Barbara Lucas
All rights reserved
Pictures copyright © 1990 by Ilon Wikland
Originally published in Sweden by Rabén & Sjögren
under the title *Visst är Lotta en glad unge,*
text copyright © 1990 by Astrid Lindgren
Library of Congress catalog card number: 90-9054
Printed in Hong Kong / Polex International AB
First edition, 1991

ISBN 91 29 59862 1

R&S Books are distributed in the United States of America
by Farrar, Straus and Giroux, New York;
in the United Kingdom by Ragged Bears, Andover;
in Canada by Vanwell Publishing, St. Catharines;
and in Australia by ERA Publications, Adelaide

Astrid Lindgren

LOTTA'S EASTER SURPRISE

Illustrated by Ilon Wikland

Translated by Barbara Lucas

R&S
BOOKS

Stockholm   New York   London   Adelaide   Toronto

"Now I'm mad," said Lotta. "I really mean it!"

She glared furiously at Jonas and Maria so they would see just how mad she was.

"That's nothing new," said Jonas.

"You're always mad."

That made Lotta even madder.

"I am not, either!" she screamed. "And you are the dumbest person there is. And Maria, too!"

Mostly, Lotta didn't think that Jonas and Maria were especially dumb. But today! Hadn't Lotta waited almost the whole morning for them to come home from school for Easter vacation? And hadn't they promised that Lotta and Maria and Jonas would dress up as Easter witches, all three of them, and go around to everybody on their street and sing for them and maybe get candy, as Easter witches always do?

Yes, they had promised! And then they come home instead and say that somebody named Kim has invited both of them to a birthday party today.

"So we can't be Easter witches until afterwards," said Maria.

Afterwards! What that meant was that Lotta would have to wait, and wait, and wait even more, while they sat and ate cake at that Kim's house. No wonder Lotta was mad!

"Don't be sad, Lotta," said Maria, and patted Lotta on the cheek. "We'll be home soon."

And they left.

Lotta stood at the gate. She was alone, and sad, and mad. But after a while she wasn't mad anymore, strangely enough, just alone and sad. And then, a little later, she wasn't even sad anymore, just alone. That's when she started to wonder what she could do until Jonas and Maria came home. She was good at finding things to do.

9

First, she took a swing through the kitchen to see what Mom was doing. Mom stood on a stepladder, hanging up clean curtains.

"What are you doing, little Lotta?" asked Mom.

"Nothing," said Lotta. "What are you doing?"

"Putting up clean curtains for Easter, as you can plainly see," said Mom.

"Does that have to be done?" asked Lotta.

"It's not a matter of have-to," said Mom. "I just think it's nice to. The Easter bunny thinks so, too, when he comes with his eggs."

Lotta felt herself grow happy when she thought about the Easter bunny. He usually hid eggs for Jonas and Maria and Lotta around the bushes in the garden. The eggs were full of chocolate and caramel, and Dad always said, "Go ahead and stuff yourselves, but don't blame me if you get a stomachache."

Lotta never blamed Dad. Anyway, it was the Easter bunny who brought the candy. He came sneaking around on Easter morning while everyone was asleep. No one saw the Easter bunny, ever, only the nice eggs that he left behind in the bushes.

Lotta ran out to the garden to see what good hiding places there might be for the Easter bunny to use. That way, she could run straight to the right places ahead of Jonas and Maria, when Dad shouted, "Ready, set, go!" on Easter morning, and the hunt began.

Lotta found a whole bunch of hiding places, and one that was especially good.

I would hide an egg right under that bush if I were the Easter bunny, she thought, and she decided that she would rush straight there as fast as she could when the time came.

Then Lotta went to see Mrs. Berg. She lived in the house next door, and Lotta went to visit her every day. Mrs. Berg was a little frail and had trouble breathing sometimes.

"How's your asthma?" asked Lotta politely.

Mrs. Berg usually complained all the time about her asthma. That was why she couldn't breathe very well.

"Thank you," said Mrs. Berg, "it's not too bad. But, Lotta dear, I believe I left my best glasses out in the toolshed. Would you go and see if you can find them?"

"Sure," said Lotta. "That way, you can save your breath." Mrs. Berg started breathing hard even if she had to walk only the short way out to the shed.

But I can walk as far as I want without getting out of breath at all, thought Lotta with satisfaction.

She went out to the shed and found the glasses right away. They were up on a trunk that stood way back in a corner behind Mrs. Berg's old bike and a whole pile of rakes and hoes and shovels and empty juice jars and bottles and other stuff that Mrs. Berg had in her shed.

"What would I do without you?" said Mrs. Berg when she took her glasses.

"I don't know," said Lotta. "It's lucky for you that I can come here and see to things a little."

Then Lotta took a swing down the
street. She thought she might meet
Jonas and Maria.

By now, they surely must have
finished up the cake.

But there wasn't any sign of Jonas
or Maria.

That's just like them, Lotta thought.
But I can go and look in Vasilis's
window in the meantime.

Vasilis had a candy store, and right
now, just before Easter, he would
surely have the shop filled with Easter
eggs, Lotta thought. Who knows,
maybe the Easter bunny bought his
eggs there.

The door stood open and Lotta peeked in. There sat Vasilis on a box, and that was all there was in the whole shop.

"Where is all the candy?" said Lotta.

"Gone," said Vasilis. "I have closed."

Vasilis cried, and Lotta started to cry, too.

"I have sold everything," said Vasilis.

"But where can we buy our Saturday candies, then?" asked Lotta.

"Ah, I don't know," said Vasilis. "Not in my shop, anyway. I am going home to Greece. You don't eat enough candy in this country. There are only Saturday candies and Saturday candies, and I can't live on that."

Lotta started crying again, and then Vasilis said, "Don't cry! I have sold the shop to an old woman who sells toys. Won't that be fun?"

But Lotta didn't want to have to choose between candy and toys just now. She was sad because Vasilis was moving back to Greece.

"Don't cry," said Vasilis. "You are always such a happy kid." He got up from the box.

"Look at this," he said, and opened the lid.

Lotta stopped crying. "What's that?" she said. That was all she could say.

"Just look," said Vasilis. "Santas and Christmas angels and marzipan pigs and snowmen, enough for fourteen Christmases. But it's not Christmas now, it's Easter." He broke into a Santa Claus so that the red foil paper came apart and Lotta could see the chocolate inside.

"Easter!" said Vasilis. "Nobody buys a single Santa Claus, do you understand, Lotta. Do you want them? You can have the whole lot."

Lotta thought Vasilis was joking.

"Will the Santas go with you to Greece?" she asked.

"I don't want to see another Santa as long as I live," said Vasilis. "You can have them."

Lotta still thought he was teasing her.

"Take them," said Vasilis. "Otherwise, I'll just have to throw them in the garbage."

At last Lotta understood that a miracle had happened.

Vasilis put the Santa Clauses and the Christmas angels and the marzipan pigs and the snowmen in two large paper bags. Lotta lifted the bags to see if she could carry that much, and she could, even though they were very heavy.

"Goodbye, Vasilis!" said Lotta. "I am so sad that you are going home to Greece."

"But I am not sad," said Vasilis. "Farewell, then. You have always been a happy little kid. Don't ever stop."

Lotta struggled up the street with her bags.

She thought and she thought. What a huge surprise this would be at home. How amazed Jonas and Maria would be!

But, thought Lotta, not quite yet. She wanted to take her own Santas out, not just let Jonas and Maria jump on the bags. Where could Lotta hide them? Jonas and Maria might come home from the cake party any time now.

Then she had an idea. Mrs. Berg's toolshed! There had to be a hiding place

there. Mrs. Berg was probably napping, as she usually did at this time of the afternoon.

Lotta plodded along toward the shed. Now she was puffing almost as much as Mrs. Berg. The bags were really heavy. But soon, soon Lotta would have them where she wanted them.

Then the worst possible thing happened.

"Lotta, where are you?"

Lotta heard Maria yelling from far away.

"Lotta, where are you?" she heard once again. Now it was Jonas shouting. Lotta looked around wildly and left her bags behind a bush. She ran to the fence and scrambled over quickly to her own back yard. Then she raced over to her swing.

"Here I am!" she called out. "What do you want?"

"We're getting dressed up as Easter witches now," Jonas shouted.

"So-o-o," cried out Lotta. "You can go without me!"

That brought them running, Jonas and Maria.

"So this is where you are," said Jonas.

"And you're still mad at us, I guess," said Maria. "Come on, Lotta, we have to go now."

"Not me," said Lotta.

"You're so stubborn," said Jonas. "Why are you still sulking?"

"I am not sulking at all," said Lotta. "I am always very happy, that's what Vasilis says. But I don't want to come with you and be an Easter witch."

"Don't, then," said Jonas. "Come on, Maria."

Off they ran, and Lotta was alone.

She was in a hurry. Quickly she climbed back over the fence, and quickly she got her bags from behind the bushes and raced across to the shed with them.

At last! Now where could she hide them? She looked around. What about that big trunk?

She lifted the lid. Only a pile of old clothes. Across the top lay a piece of black, shiny cloth.

"You can lie comfortably here," said Lotta, and she dropped her Santas and angels and marzipan pigs and snowmen on top of the black cloth. They looked wonderful, she thought. She could hardly tear herself away from them.

But she had to hurry.

Jonas and Maria were running around making themselves into Easter witches when Lotta rushed up.

"All right, then. I'll come with you," she said.

"Oh, so you're not mad anymore?" said Jonas.

"No, I'm happy!" said Lotta, and a tickling, pleasant little shiver went through her when she thought about the trunk.

"Three truly sweet Easter witches," said Mrs. Berg. She looked out her window just as the Easter witches walked by.

"Are you finally awake?" called Lotta. How lucky that Mrs. Berg had slept for such a long time!

"Yes, I am," said Mrs. Berg. "But I don't have any candy to give you today."

No candy! That was what they had heard everywhere they went.

"There have been so many Easter witches," said one man. "The candy is all gone. You came too late!"

Jonas and Maria looked glum.

"It's because you went to eat cake," said Lotta.

Then she quietly said to herself, "Please don't let me tell them what I have in the trunk!"

It was almost impossible to keep such secret. But Lotta buttoned up her mouth and said nothing.

Jonas and Maria took off their skirts and shawls and aprons and kerchiefs as soon as they came inside. Absolutely never would they be Easter witches again! Only Lotta sat like a little rosy, contented Easter witch at the dinner table.

Dad had also come home, but he seemed a little troubled.

"Can you imagine?" he said to Mom. "Vasilis has gone out of business. I couldn't buy any Easter eggs because the shop was closed."

"Oh, no," said Mom. "How will the Easter bunny get his eggs, then?"

"Tomorrow, all the shops will be closed because it is Good Friday," said Dad. "I'll have to go into the city on Saturday to buy them. That means the Easter bunny won't come on time this year."

"That's dumb," said Maria. "We always hunt for Easter eggs first thing in the morning!"

Lotta didn't say anything; she didn't understand. Couldn't the Easter bunny take care of his own eggs? What did Dad have to do with it?

After dinner she asked Jonas, and he laughed. "Don't you understand that Dad is the Easter bunny? He is also Santa, if you want to know."

No, Lotta didn't want to know that at all. An Easter bunny should be a real Easter bunny, and Santa Claus should be a real Santa. That was what made it so exciting and mysterious when it was Christmas and Easter. Dad was always good to have around, but Lotta didn't want to have him all mixed up with the Easter bunny and the real Santa.

Lotta felt herself get sad. What a terrible Easter it would be without Easter eggs and without the real Easter bunny.

She had to think about this for a while.

Lotta thought.

Mrs. Berg slept late the next morning as well. Otherwise, she might have seen someone coming out of the toolshed, someone in blue pajamas, with two huge bags, one in each hand.

But nobody was awake, not even the Nymans in the little yellow house.

When Lotta was finished with the strange thing that she was going to do that morning, she crept back into her lovely bed and slept.

Jonas and Maria were already up and all dressed when Lotta woke up. "Come on, Lotta," said Maria. "Maybe the Easter bunny came, after all."

"Yeah. Otherwise, it will be a terrible Easter," said Jonas.

Lotta didn't say anything. She just smiled a little to herself.

Maria helped her get dressed so they could go outside quicker.

Mom and Dad sat in the kitchen, drinking coffee.

"Did the Easter bunny come here, after all?" asked Maria.

"Maria, you know he didn't," said Mom.

"You know he'll come tomorrow instead," said Dad.

Maria's mouth went into a pout. "Tomorrow isn't the same," she said.

"It should be the way it always is," said Jonas.

Lotta went to the door. "I think I'll just take a look, in any case."

And she disappeared.

Dad was trying to comfort Jonas and Maria when they heard Lotta's happy cry from the garden.

"Come and see something strange!" cried Lotta.

Jonas and Maria ran out. There stood Lotta pointing eagerly at something in the grass over by the birch.

Something unbelievable.

"Oh, no, now I think Dad has gone completely crazy," said Jonas.

The green grass was full of red Santas and white angels and marzipan pigs and snowmen.

They looked as if they were having a wonderful time together, as if they were getting ready to play.

Jonas and Maria started to laugh.

"All of them are chocolate," said Jonas.

"Except the marzipan pigs," said Maria.

Now Mom and Dad came out, too.

"What is this?" said Dad. "Where did all this come from?"

Maria laughed. "You are the one who said the Easter bunny wouldn't come!"

"And he didn't come, either," said Lotta. "A little Christmas bunny came, instead!" She giggled so hard that she could barely stand up.

"I don't know anything about this," said Dad.

"I don't, either," said Mom.

"Me, either," said Lotta.

She started to giggle again and she thought how much she would love to surprise them every day. Then she re-membered what she had left in the trunk, a Santa, an angel, a marzipan pig, and a snowman. But she wasn't going to make any surprises with them.

"I am a happy kid, that's what Vasilis said, and right now I am especially happy," said Lotta.

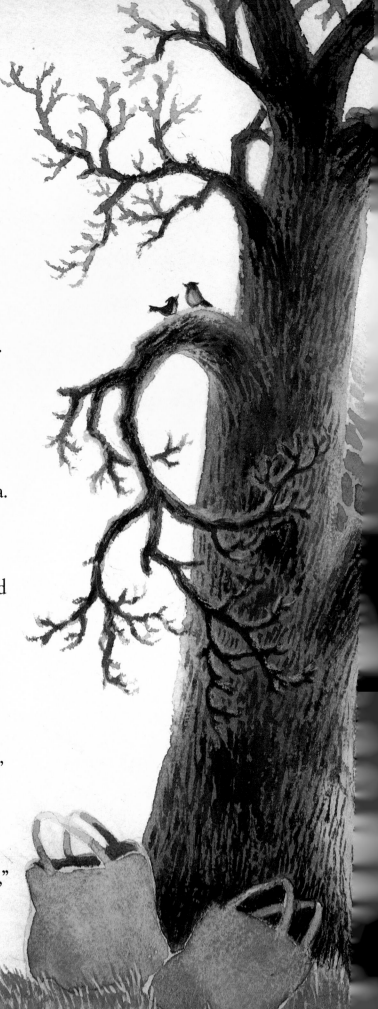